P9-DZM-337

CARLOTTA'S SECRET

Look for the full series of Patricia Canterbury Mysteries:

Also:

POPLAR COVE MYSTERIES:

CARLOTTA'S SECRET

by
Patricia E. Canterbury

ISBN 0-9703178-3-2

Copyright © 2000 Patricia E. Canterbury

Published by Ramona's Book Company

Division of RBC Publishing Co, Inc.

All rights reserved.

Printed in the U.S.A.

Cover design and illustrations by Donna M. Orth

Patricia Canterbury's photo by Jon Stevenson

Book design and typesetting by Sue Knopf

Library of Congress Catalog Number 2001086589

Acknowledgments

To the ZICA Creative Arts & Literary Guild Member who wrote the phrase, "There was something about the way she said 'Welcome' that . . ."

To the weekly writers' critique group: Maggie Anderson, Ethel Mack Ballard, Jacqueline Turner Banks, Terris McMahan Grimes and Geri Spencer Hunter for their enthusiasm in the development of Carlotta and Webster Street Gang.

Thanks to my editor, Sandy Ferguson Fuller, and Donna Orth, my illustrator, for the wonderful job they did in making my novel "come to life."

To my husband, Richard,
for reading countless rewrites and edits.

Contents

CHAPTER ONE

Willow Springs and Me

There was something in the way she said "Welcome" that should have told me to turn around and run as far away as possible. But I didn't dare. I stood just outside her door looking over at the Webster Street Gang and, especially, Timmy Johnson. I could see Timmy smiling, waiting for me to turn tail and run. I could also hear him saying, "Just what you'd expect from a girl," one of his favorite phrases. I knew that if I ran away, I'd never be welcomed into the neighborhood club. My six new friends, Timmy, Margo Goldstein, Lewis and Randy Williams, Tru Nguyen, and Monroe Jones, who call themselves the Webster Street Gang, a name they chose after seeing a Disney movie, were still making me prove that I was really one of them.

They thought that adding "Gang" to their name made them seem tough and strong when they play baseball. They're really good. I think that they could beat the Regional Champions. For the past six years, kids from a tiny school in Galt, California, have beat the stuffings out of the Webster Street Gang and every other baseball team from Willow Springs. But that was before I came to town.

Ever since my parents moved to Willow Springs four weeks ago, I'd been trying to make friends. Willow Springs is a really nice, quiet delta town. It's right on the banks of the Sacramento River. At first I didn't think that I would like it 'cuz I'm from New York City. New York's really busy and filled with lots of people. Here in Willow Springs, you can walk down blocks and blocks of tree-shaded streets and hardly see anyone but retired people sitting on their porches or walking their dogs.

I'm used to subways and taxis and hardly ever walked anyplace in New York. I walk everywhere here in Willow Springs. I'm learning to like walking. Willow Springs' population is barely 3,000. There must have been almost 3,000 kids just in my elementary school in New York. Still Willow Springs has its own charm, as Mom tells Aunt Alicia when they talk on the telephone every day.

Willow Springs is close to Sacramento, California's state capital. Mom and Dad can drive to Sacramento in less than a half hour if they take the freeway. It takes longer if they use the levee road. The levee road is a crooked, narrow road that runs along the side of the Sacramento River between the river to the west and the pear farms to the east. I never knew there were so many pears as there are growing around Willow Springs.

Anyway, I was telling you about standing in front of Miss Simon's door. Miss Simon's backyard is next to the vacant lot where I play baseball with my new friends. This morning, standing on her porch waiting for her to open the door, all I can think of is the first time I met my friends.

But to continue with the information about the Webster Street Gang. They stood on Miss Simon's lawn staring at me, waiting for me to make up my mind. Usually I'm a pretty outgoing kid. Usually I can make up my mind, awfully fast. I had to in New York 'cuz while you're standing on the platform deciding which subway train to take, the right one would have come and gone and left you standing there stranded. I'm pretty smart, too, according to my folks and teachers. But I could tell from the smiles on the Webster Street Gang's faces that I still had to prove myself to them. Not all the kids in Willow Springs were making me prove myself, just the six who lived on my street.

I don't know what they expected of me. Just because I'm from New York it doesn't make me a monster or anything. Luckily Margo, the only other girl in the Webster Street Gang, was really fun and was the first to invite me to join.

CHAPTER TWO

Margo and Mom

"Hi, my name's Margo Goldstein. I live across the street in the green house." A young girl with coarse auburn hair petted Spot, my mostly black cat, and helped me bring a lamp from the moving van into my new house. She was the first person I met in Willow Springs. I liked her right away. She sort of reminded me of Mrs. Steinberg, my violin teacher. Margo has the same curly hair and pale skin as Mrs. Steinberg.

"I play the piano," Margo said, as I carried my violin case inside.

"I'm Carlotta Stevens. I'm from New York," I said, following her.

"Wow, New York, I've never met anyone from New York. Maybe we could play together at the school recital. I also play baseball, Mom doesn't like it that I play ball. She's afraid that I'll hurt my hands. Can you play baseball?" Margo's sentences ran together like she was thinking of the next thing to say before she finished her last thought. I'd just met her and knew that someday she was going to be my almost best friend.

"Uh-huh. I play first base. My mom's afraid I'll hurt my fingers, too. But I'm very good and hardly ever hurt myself."

"I'm a good player, too. First base, that's my position. You can play second base," Margo teased, pushing her hair out of her blue eyes. I noticed that she bit her fingernails. None of my New York friends bit their fingernails.

"Mom, this is Margo, she lives across the street in the green house," I announced, pointing to the only green house on our block.

"Pleased to meet you, Margo." Mom smiled and turned toward the two movers walking into the kitchen carrying boxes labeled "kitchen stuff."

"Ma'am, this is the last box," one of the movers said, lowering a large box to the floor near the box covered table.

"Put the kitchen things down first while I make you some coffee," Mom said, plugging in the coffee maker above the dark-blue tile counter.

"Carlotta, dear, please stay out of the way. Why don't you and Margo go outside to play. The juice in the fridge is cold; take a carton and a couple of oranges from the kitchen table. It's a beautiful day and you're getting in the movers' way." Mom walked past us and opened two boxes before finding the one with the coffee mugs.

"Thanks, Mrs. Stevens. Come on Carlotta, you can play second base. We need someone who can throw. You can throw, can't you? Timmy doesn't think any girl can throw," Margo said, biting into one of the fresh oranges.

"Who's Timmy?" I asked.

"He's the leader of the Webster Street Gang."

"Webster Street Gang?"

"Uh-huh. We all live on this street and we play baseball." Margo walked out of the kitchen just ahead of the movers.

"Mrs. Stevens, you could invite the Gang over for lemonade and Carlotta could get to know them."

"The Gang?"

"Yes, Mom, they play baseball just like the kids in New York," I said.

"I guess it'll be okay. But first, we have to unpack or everyone will be drinking lemonade out of paper cups." Mom hates paper cups. She's taught me all about real china and silver-ware and other things.

Two days later the Webster Street Gang came over for lemonade.

CHAPTER THREE

The Webster Street Gang and Me

"Mom, this is Timmy Johnson." Timmy, a long-legged eleven-year-old boy, shook Mom's hand. He was nearly as tall as Mom with about the same color skin. Timmy has tiny dreadlocks about an inch long all over his head. I think they're cute. Mom doesn't like them. She wears her long black hair in thick braids that cover her ears. Mom and I used to wear our hair the same way but last year I began wearing braids all over my head. My hair is dark brown with red highlights, like Dad's. I look like my Dad except for my hairstyle.

Timmy and the rest of the Gang stood around our lawn furniture in our backyard, under a valley oak. Mom brought out six glasses and two tall pitchers of fresh-squeezed lemonade. Mom doesn't like to serve lemonade from cans. She says that hand-squeezed lemons are "sweeter."

"Pleased to meet you, Mrs. Stevens," Timmy said, his voice breaking a little. He smiled, embarrassed by his voice. I think his voice is cute. He ignored me and tossed a baseball over to Tru.

"Pleased to meet you, Timmy." Mom smiled.

"This is Tru Nguyen. His grandfather was born in Vietnam," I said.

"Hi," Tru said, pushing his coal-black hair out of his dark eyes and tossing the baseball back to Timmy. He's skinny like Timmy and usually wears the same kind of cut-off Levi's as Timmy and Monroe.

"Mom, this is Monroe Jones. He has a swimming pool." I introduced him and poured myself a glass of lemonade. Monroe was having his second glass of lemonade and his first handful of cookies.

"Hi," Monroe said, with a mouthful of chocolate chip cookie. Mom bought the cookies. She doesn't make good cookies but she bakes wonderful pies.

"Your parents have a swimming pool?" Mom asked, just to be polite.

"Yes, but I can't let anyone come over to swim unless Mom or Dad are at home." Monroe washed the cookie down with a glass of lemonade. Monroe likes to eat and he never gains a pound, unlike me who still has most of my baby fat.

"Sounds like you have good, caring parents," Mom said, walking back into the house.

"Is Lewis coming over?" I asked, looking through the picket fence on the side of the house. I could just see part of Webster Street where it crosses Pine. Lewis and Randy live at the corner of Webster and Pine in a two-story brick house with dark green shutters.

"Lewis? Yeah, he's always late," Margo said, climbing up to the lowest branch of the oak tree. "He'll be over in a few minutes. I bet I can climb higher than anyone." She pulled a large branch down so she could walk on it to the next higher branch.

"Yeah, he's always late," Randy echoed, throwing the baseball to Timmy. Randy and Lewis are as different as two brothers can be. Lewis is eleven months older. They were born in the same year, one in January and the other in December. They look like twins except Lewis wears glasses and is a better batter.

We were all still in the backyard oak tree when Lewis arrived.

"Mom told me to bring your mom this casserole." Lewis pushed his round glasses up on his nose and put a covered glass dish on the lawn table. He jumped up to the bottom branch.

"You were supposed to wait for me," Lewis said, punching Randy on his left arm.

"You're always late." Randy said, punching him back. They reminded me of the Morelli brothers who lived above the deli next to our apartment house in New York. Marco and Gus Morelli were in my homeroom class in New York. They were always punching each other. I guess my friends right here in Willow Springs aren't any different.

"Kids, don't climb too high. I don't want anyone falling," Mom called from the kitchen window.

"We won't. Mom, Lewis and Randy's mother sent over a casserole."

"Thank you, boys, I'll bring out some plates and forks."

When Mom came outside, she noticed Lewis's skinned knees and torn socks. Lewis's clothes were always a mess because he took off his glasses whenever he had to run and he slid into

15

bases and people all the time. He refused to wear his glasses when he played baseball. He was our best player.

Randy always looked like he never got dirty, but he never stole bases either.

"When you've finished with lunch, kids, come inside," Mom said. "I rented the latest *Star Wars* video." She passed the Mom test and was accepted right away.

CHAPTER FOUR

Dad, a Town Leader

"Linda, it was kind of funny the way he said it," Dad said to Mom over dinner a few days later.

"What was funny, Dad?"

"Lawrence Marks, the head of the Rotary, is a funny man."

"What's a Rotary?" I asked.

"It's a service organization, dear. The members do good things for the town."

"Like what?"

"They raise money for the new hospital wing or for the school library."

"I like the library. It has almost as many books as the library in our old neighborhood," I said, half-listening to Dad's conversation. Mom was serving potato salad and a fresh mixed peas and carrot salad. We eat a lot of salad in the summer.

Dad kept talking. "Lawrence said, 'Harry, my son, I want you to join the Willow Springs Country Club. I'll sponsor you.'"

"The Country Club? What did you tell him?"

"I told him no. Said I didn't want to be the token banker." Mom and Dad laughed.

"Well dear, you *are* the new bank president. People will expect you to join the Chamber of Commerce, and the United Way, and the Country Club. Everyone's going to want to wine and dine you. I guess you'll just have to grin and bear it," Mom said, pouring a second glass of mint ice tea.

"I told him that I'm not much of a joiner. He just laughed and said that he and his wife would pick us up for dinner Saturday. Wants to show us the sights in Sacramento."

"Oh, dear, Sacramento. Isn't that awfully far to go for dinner?"

"I guess not. Californians think nothing of driving a hundred miles for dinner."

"Wow, is Sacramento a hundred miles from here?" I asked, suddenly very interested in Mom and Dad's conversation.

"No, pumpkin, it's only thirty-five miles or so."

"I've read all about the Gold Rush and stuff. Are you going to Sutter's Fort? I'd like to go to Sutter's Fort."

"I think we're going to a restaurant on the Downtown Mall. I can't remember the name of it."

"Can we go to Sutter's Fort?" I asked.

"Yes, maybe next week. I'll leave the office early and the three of us will go to Sutter's Fort."

"Daddy, did Mr. Marks really call you Harry? Didn't you tell him that your name is Harrison?"

"Yes. I've repeatedly told him my name. Folks out here in California shorten everyone's name. I'm just Harry to most of the people I've met."

"Nobody—not even Mom—calls you Harry. You've been called Harrison for ages, even before I was born."

"That's right, pumpkin, even before you were born."

CHAPTER FIVE

Miss Simon—the Witch

But I was talking about the Witch, wasn't I? I did mention her, didn't I?

Summer vacation had begun the Saturday before we moved to Willow Springs. I was looking forward to three whole months of summer to get to know my new sixth grade classmates.

"Can I play on the team?" I asked Timmy, the day after the Gang came over for lunch.

"I guess so, even if you *are* a girl." Margo was right—Timmy Johnson is very fond of saying that whenever Margo and I are involved in anything with the rest of the Webster Street Gang. Like there's something wrong with being a girl.

"You can practice with Randy and Monroe," Timmy said. Margo and I were stuck with those members of the Gang who would rather play soccer or swim than play baseball. We just had to show the whole team that we were as good as Timmy, Lewis or Tru. Maybe even better.

"Girls can't throw," Timmy announced during morning practice, just before I threw him out at second base.

"Wow, did you see that?" Tru asked, standing behind home base waiting for Timmy to walk to the bench. I could hear the admiration in Tru's voice.

"Yeah, I saw her." Timmy grumbled.

I made him swallow those words. I don't know why it's so important for Timmy to like me. Maybe it's because he's sorta cute. He's all legs and skinned knees and his full lips have a kind of crooked way of smiling whenever he laughs. Margo was right about something else— Timmy is the leader of the Webster Street Gang. He is the one who organizes the baseball games, or follow the leader, or skateboarding or swimming.

Okay, I really was accepted, but I still had to prove myself worthy of being a real member the Webster Street Gang. But I want to tell you about the Witch . . .

"If you want to be one of us you've got to ring Miss Simon's bell. She's a witch." Timmy said one Saturday morning.

"She's a what?" I asked, not really believing my ears.

"You heard right. Miss Simon is a witch. The whole town knows it." Monroe said it this time, for once talking without eating at the same time. He always carries apples around the way most kids carry candy bars. I've never seen him eat a candy bar.

"I . . . I can't believe that you expect me to think that you have a real witch living in Willow Springs," I said, trying to sound really grown-up and New-York-like. "Your own Miss Simon."

"She's not *my* Miss Simon. She really is a witch. She turned the Andersens' prize bull into a toad," Randy bragged, his cheeks flushed with excitement.

"Really, did you see her do that?" I asked. "I've never seen anyone turn a bull or anything else into a toad. Not even in New York."

"No, but we know she did it. One minute the Andersens' bull was standing in the pasture and the next minute, he was gone. Turned into a toad. We all saw the toad."

"Yeah, we all saw the toad," Tru and Lewis echoed.

CHAPTER SIX

Ringing Miss Simon's Doorbell

"Well, okay, I'll ring her doorbell, but all of you are going to have to come with me. I'm not going up to her house by myself," I said.

"Oh, we're going with you. If you really, really

want to be part of the Gang you have to walk up the steps and ring the bell and . . ." Timmy paused.

"Do I have to talk to her?" I asked.

"Uh . . . Oh, no, we've never talked to her," Tru said, his dark eyes flashing. Timmy, Lewis, Monroe and Randy took a step back from me.

Margo walked closer to me and whispered, "Carlotta, it's just a silly boys' game. Don't let them know you're scared. I was so nervous when I rang Miss Simon's bell that I almost wet my pants. But they don't know that."

I gave Margo's hand a squeeze and walked up the dark blue steps to Miss Simon's porch. The Webster Street Gang often played in the vacant lot behind Miss Simon's house. But I'd never been closer to her house than the fence separating it from the baseball diamond. I rang the bell. My heart pounded so hard I was sure that my friends could hear it. The door opened and Miss Simon was standing in front of me waiting for me to say something.

"Welcome," she said, opening the door wide. She remained inside, holding the door open. I could smell her perfume. Like fresh vanilla.

Now, I grew up in New York City. I've ridden the subway all over the city, I've attended night concerts in Central Park with my folks, I've taken the train to Connecticut to visit my grandparents and once I flew on a plane by myself, to Arizona, to visit my other grandparents. So I wasn't going to let any small-town witch stop me from being a real part of the Webster Street Gang.

Still, there was something about the way she said "Welcome" that made my flesh crawl. I stood on the porch, she stood inside the house, holding the screen door open. The house smelled as good as she did, sort of like bread baking.

"Welcome, children, why don't you all come inside?" She stepped back into the bright, breezy room, making space for me.

"We'd love to," I said. New Yorkers are always polite. I walked back down the steps and grabbed Margo with one hand and Timmy with the other, and walked back up to the porch and into the house. Randy, Monroe, Lewis and Tru slowly followed us. Don't ask me why.

CHAPTER SEVEN

Iced Tea and Me

"Iced tea and cookies, children?" Miss Simon asked. We nodded, too scared to say anything. She didn't look like a witch to me. She was pretty in a Vanessa Williams, the former Miss America, sort of way, except her hair was cut real short. She wasn't thin like witches are supposed to be. She was really curvy like I'd like to be when I grow up.

Only I'll probably be chubby like Mom. Chubby's okay. Mom gets lots of admiring looks. I heard Dad tell her so. I heard him say, "Linda, you're just perfect, you get lots of admiring looks." Then Mom blushed and hugged him and baked us a fresh lemon meringue pie.

But I was telling you about Miss Simon. She walked in front of us into the dining room.

"Sit here, children." She pointed to the dining room table with eight matching chairs.

The Webster Street Gang and I sat down. The table was real pretty cherry wood, with a white lace tablecloth and fresh hothouse sweet peas in a Lenox vase placed right in the center. I'm from New York. I know about furniture and hothouse plants and fancy china. Mom told me I needed to know those things so that when I visit people I will have something to talk about besides what's on television. Speaking of television, Miss Simon turned hers on.

"My favorite program. I don't miss it even when I have company. Make yourselves comfortable, children. I'll be right back." She changed the channel to the sci-fi station. Something about *Tales from the Darkside*® was just beginning. But no one paid any attention to the TV. Our eyes were glued to Miss Simon's every move as she walked from the dining room into the kitchen. We could see the entire kitchen from where we sat. She opened the refrigerator and took out a pitcher of iced tea and a bucket of ice.

"The cookies should be ready now." The oven timer went off. Opening the oven door, she took out a tray of oatmeal raisin cookies.

"Can we help?" Margo asked.

"Oh, no. Stay seated." Miss Simon carried the ice bucket, pitcher and cookies on a large dark red platter into the dining room.

She poured iced tea into each of our tall glasses.

"Margo, when did she put these glasses and plates on the table?" I whispered.

"Remember, she's a witch. She can work magic," Margo whispered back, her voice trembling. Each of us took a fresh, warm cookie from the platter as Miss Simon passed it around the table. She sat at the head of the table facing the front door.

"Thank you, Miss Simon," we said, almost together. Timmy' voice cracked again. Margo and I laughed.

"We thought you were a witch," I said, my mouth full of oatmeal raisin.

"Oh? Why would anyone think I was a witch? Aren't witches ugly, horrible people who snatch little children and have them for breakfast?" she asked, laughing lightly. The Webster Street Gang and I stopped fidgeting in our chairs and looked at each other.

"Nonsense, kids. There aren't any such beings as witches," Miss Simon continued.

I rubbed my eyes.

For a second I could have sworn that as she spoke, her skin turned a putrid green, then returned to normal. I looked at each of my friends. They were enjoying eating the cookies. No one else seemed to notice. I put my half-eaten cookie down and didn't touch the iced tea.

Come on Carlotta, I said to myself, *you've been in scarier situations in New York. Think— you need to get your friends and yourself out of here.* I'd read somewhere that witches hate cloves. But I didn't have any cloves, and if she was a witch she wouldn't have any around either.

I patted my Levi's pockets and carefully placed their contents on the table next to my plate. I had my house key, a yo-yo, and catnip for Spot's dessert. Catnip—now what had I learned about catnip? No use. I seemed to have lost all of my sharp-witted New York City skills in the hazy summer days in Willow Springs.

"It's been nice having iced tea and cookies with you, Miss Simon, but we have to go . . ."

"To a baseball game," Timmy interrupted, before I could finish my sentence. I could see that he was ready to take the lead. Ready to tell all the other kids that he'd eaten at Miss Simon's and left safe and sound.

"Baseball?" Miss Simon asked, her pale skin again taking on a greenish hue.

"Uh-huh," I said. Taking Margo, who seemed mesmerized by her, by the hand and getting up, I began walking toward the door.

CHAPTER EIGHT

Miss Simon's Spell

"I'm afraid I can't let you kids leave," Miss Simon said, so softly that we barely heard her.

"What?" Lewis asked, leaning forward in his chair. He was seated next to Miss Simon on the right.

"Yes you can," I said. "You can open the door and we'll leave." Pulling Margo with me and nearly knocking over the heavy wooden chair, I ran to the door. Miss Simon was swifter. She sort of flew to the door or the wall or . . .

Randy rushed over to Lewis. Timmy and Tru hugged each other. Margo and I froze where we were in front of the space where the front door should have been.

"Where's the door?" I asked, almost hysterical, just like Timmy might expect. The door we'd just come through was gone. We were in a completely enclosed room with just the Webster Street Gang, me, and Miss Simon inside. Margo, to her credit, didn't cry, but Monroe looked like he might and he was already twelve.

"Let us out of here," Timmy shouted.

"Yes, let us out of here. You can't keep us here," Monroe added, half-choking on a cookie.

"Our parents know that we're here," Tru said, looking around the room quickly to see if anyone would back him up. Actually, our parents thought we were playing in the vacant lot just beyond our view.

Everyone was talking at once, so it was hard to know what to do next. Miss Simon was shimmering from light green to pale golden and back to green. The Webster Street Gang pounded their hands against the walls. The walls refused to budge. The floor seemed to move slightly under our feet.

"Earthquake," I yelled, trying to make myself heard above the screams.

"What?" Margo shouted.

"I feel the floor moving. Is there an earthquake?

"No, I think it's just Miss Simon. I told you that she's a real witch. Do you think she's going to try to eat us?"

"No, witches don't eat people," I said, hoping that I wouldn't eat my words!

CHAPTER NINE

Me

I told you that I grew up in New York, right? Did I also tell you that my ancestors were here when the first settlers arrived? Did I tell you that I only pretended to be afraid of Miss Simon because I'd been told that I had to be very careful? Even though Miss Simon, possibly a Martian or something equally as revolting, was not a witch.

I am.

I don't want anyone, especially not my new friends, to know my secret. No one in New York knew that Mom's a witch and Dad's a warlock. And as their true daughter, I am also a witch.

I've known that I'm a witch since I was a little, little kid. Mom and Dad had to tell me one day when, just by thinking really really hard, I made my stuffed dragon come to life. They told me that I mustn't change my toys and make them real. That I could only play with my toys like regular kids do.

I'm very smart, as I told you already. I was always very careful after that, about everything. Mom won't let me use my powers unless she's with me.

"I don't want you doing things that you can't control," she even told me again, right after we moved to Willow Springs.

"You're still learning. I didn't know what I could do until I was sixteen or seventeen. You're not quite twelve."

"Yes, Mom, I'll be careful." And I am. I hadn't used any of my magic since we'd been in Willow Springs.

But today was different. Miss Simon had made the door and windows disappear and trapped us inside her house. The beautiful dining room table, chairs, flowers, iced tea and cookies disappeared. We stood in a large, dark, windowless room with gargoyles in the corner and green smoke coming from the hidden fireplace.

The Webster Street Gang screamed and pounded on the walls. Miss Simon laughed wickedly, and rubbed her hands together.

"So, children, you think that you can ring my doorbell and eat my cookies and walk away with out so much as a thank you?" she asked, smiling.

"Oh, my gosh, look at her teeth." Tru whispered.

"Her teeth?" I asked.

"Yeah, she had beautiful white teeth, but they're turning yellow and pointy."

"Oh, you're right," I said, trying to figure out how to get my friends out of Miss Simon's reach."

"Than . . . thank . . . thank you, Miss Simon," Timmy tried to say, as politely as possible.

"It's too late. You should have thought of your manners before you began ringing the door-bell."

Monroe's bottom lip quivered, tears filled Margo's and Timmy's eyes. Lewis and Randy hugged each other. Tru and I walked toward the fireplace.

"There must be a way out," I whispered.

"There's one way out, but I'm not going to walk through the fireplace to escape. I don't think she's going to let us go," Tru said.

I moved around the room trying to distract the Gang and Miss Simon. She watched us closely, turning quickly from one kid to the other. She couldn't keep watching all of us at once. Randy and Lewis ran in one direction,

Timmy and Tru in another. Margo hid behind a chair that changed into a snarling dragon snorting red smoke.

She screamed and ran over to Monroe and Lewis.

"Miss Simon, our parents know that we're here," I repeated, making my voice stay calm.

"I heard that the first time," she snarled. "I've been watching you children. Your parents don't know that you come here and ring my doorbell. They wouldn't think that their little darlings would be so rude.

"I promise that if you let us go, we'll never ring your bell again." The rest of the Gang crossed their hearts and nodded.

Miss Simon shook her shoulders. Her short dark hair was now sticking out in razor-sharp purple spikes all over her head. Her eyes glowed yellow. Her skin remained a horrible green. She was the most awful thing I'd ever seen. I also knew that she wasn't a witch.

"Why is she turning colors like that?" Monroe asked quietly. His eyes were as big as saucers.

"Maybe she's just like the wicked witch in *The Wizard of Oz*—remember, she was green too," Margo tried, but Monroe wasn't convinced.

Miss Simon wiped her mouth with the back of her hand and grabbed Randy's left arm.

He yelled.

I yelled.

The rest of the Gang yelled.

While everyone was yelling and Miss Simon was grabbing, I thought real hard and changed the gargoyles back into the candle holders they were before Miss Simon began her magic.

"What? What's happening? Who's doing that?" Miss Simon wailed, letting go of Randy and running over to the candlesticks, picking them up and turning them over. She mumbled something I couldn't hear. The candlesticks remained candlesticks. She threw them to the floor, breaking them in half.

"Who's doing what?" I asked.

"You children put my things back the way they were. I'm in charge here."

"Are you?" Margo asked.

"Margo, we have to get the boys out of here." I turned to her again, taking her hand and walking slowly toward the front wall.

"How are we going to do that?" Margo asked.

"I think Miss Simon's magic is leaving her. Maybe she can't work her magic with lots of kids near her. Quick, follow me, I think the door is over here. I saw the space where the door used to be shimmer and shake for a second when Miss Simon grabbed Randy."

"Quick, boys, follow us," Margo and I yelled, as we rushed toward the space. For once the boys listened, and in a line we burst outside into the bright sunshine.

CHAPTER TEN

Who's Going to Tell?

Miss Simon didn't know who to blame. She knew that one, or possibly more, of the Webster Street Gang, was her equal and more.

Screaming with the rest, I had run outside and pretended to be scared.

"I told you that she was a witch," Timmy said, "I wasn't scared. I just pretended to be scared to throw her off base. I knew that we'd get away from her. We're the Webster Street Gang." He tossed his baseball over to Tru.

"Well *I* was scared. I thought she was going to eat us," Lewis said, removing his glasses and wiping them on his dirty shirttail.

"So was I," Monroe admitted.

"So was I," I said, and Margo nodded.

"I knew you girls would be scared," Timmy teased, smiling at us.

"I wonder how she did the things she did? Why did she change things back? Was she just pretending to keep us in the dungeon?" Randy asked.

"No, I think that she couldn't focus on all of us at once, so she let us go. I don't know about the rest of you, but I'm not going anywhere near her again," I said.

"My mom isn't going to believe a word of this. Grownups don't believe in witches," Margo said.

"I'm not going to tell my mom. She wouldn't

let me come out and play ball for a week if she knew we'd rung Miss Simon's doorbell. Mom doesn't like me to do things like that," Timmy said.

"We'd get in trouble too," Lewis and Randy agreed.

My secret was safe.

CHAPTER ELEVEN

Finally a Member

"Carlotta, you're really a member of the Webster Street Gang, now. You proved that you can be teased, just like a boy. Plus you're brave," Timmy said, sticking out his chest like he'd just paid her a compliment.

"Thanks, Timmy."

We were always very careful after that whenever we played near Miss Simon's house. I knew we had nothing to be afraid of. She was afraid of us. She knew that at least one of us could see her for her true self.

Once I went back to her house alone and peeked into her living room windows. I saw her again up close. She was really revolting when you saw what she actually was. I don't know what she is, but she's green and moldy when she's not wearing makeup. She's really good with makeup! She knew that all real witches are golden brown and catlike.

"Miss Simon's not half as interesting as you, Mom," I said, after I returned home that day.

"Oh, who's Miss Simon? I don't think I've met her," Mom said, planting fresh flower bulbs in the flower bed under the front windows. We'd have lots of daffodils in the spring.

"She's a Martian, or something equally revolting," I said.

"Carlotta, you know that there's no such

thing as Martians. Now, go out and play with your friends."

"But she is, Mom, really."

"Carlotta. What did I tell you about making up stories about people? I'm sure Miss Simon's just a lonely woman who minds her own business."

"I guess. Mom, you know that I just want to be a regular kid and play baseball, swim and go skateboarding. Don't you?"

"Yes, I know, honey. What brought this on? You haven't been changing your toys again, have you?"

"No." I decided not to tell her any more. I left Mom planting bulbs as I walked down Webster Street toward the baseball diamond.

"Hello, Miss Simon," I said, as I walked past her house. She was actually sitting out on her front porch, wearing lots of makeup.

"Go away," she said, rushing back into her house and slamming the door.

"Did you notice that Miss Simon goes inside whenever we come by?" Monroe asked a few days later on our way to the baseball field.

"She only goes inside when Carlotta comes by," Tru said.

"I think she's afraid of you, Carlotta," Timmy agreed, after formally inviting me to join the Webster Street Gang.

"Yeah, Carlotta, Miss Simon's afraid of you," Lewis, Randy, Monroe, Tru and Margo said, at different times, in different ways.

"Me? Why would a witch be afraid of me?" I asked, then I winked at Timmy.

"I'm *just* a girl."